Bobo Starts a Band

A BOBO BOOK

AuthorHouse™
1663 Liberty Drive
Bloomington, IN 47403
www.authorhouse.com
Phone: 1 (800) 839-8640

Published by AuthorHouse 06/30/2018

ISBN: 978-1-5462-4514-8 (sc)
ISBN: 978-1-5462-4515-5 (e)
ISBN: 978-1-5462-4513-1 (hc)

Library of Congress Control Number: 2018906561

Print information available on the last page.

Any people depicted in stock imagery provided by Getty Images are models,
and such images are being used for illustrative purposes only.
Certain stock imagery © Getty Images.

This book is printed on acid-free paper.

authorHOUSE®

This is a story about our grandpa.

He may be different from your grandpa but
he <u>always</u> makes us feel special.

We call him BoBo.

BoBo Starts a Band

A BoBo Book

Megan Burton

Illustrated by Dominic Wolocko

Hi!

My name is Lizzie and this is my brother, Alex.

While most people have a grandpa to visit, we have BoBo.

One Sunday afternoon we walked over to BoBo's
house to see what he was up to.

"What are you doing BoBo?" we asked.

"I want to clean out the garage today," he answered.

BoBo was right... the garage was a mess!
There were gardening tools, bikes, shovels,
and boxes <u>EVERYWHERE</u>!

7

"BoBo, we can help you clean up. Where should we start?"

"Great! Start in the corner while I move this trash can," he answered.

Suddenly, we heard a noise... "TAP! TAP!"

Again... "TAP! TAP!"

Louder... "TAP! TAP!"

TAP!

We turned around and found BoBo playing the trash can like a drum and singing this song:

March! March!
March to the beat!

March! March!
Move those feet!

"Here we go!" I said.

Alex looked around and found an old bike horn and
I picked up a rake from the messy garage.

BoBo's band now had a drum, a trumpet, and a guitar.

March! March!
March to **the beat!**

March! March!
Move those **feet!**

As we started to play, BoBo's neighbors came out of their houses to see what was causing so much noise.

Before we knew it, the whole neighborhood wanted to join us! Norah grabbed a garden shovel and Tyler picked up a pool inner tube.

BoBo's band now had a drum, a trumpet, a guitar, a flute, and a tuba.

March! March!
March to the beat!

March! March!
Move those feet!

Adam found two empty boxes and Josie picked up an old bird feeder.

BoBo's band now had a drum, a trumpet, a guitar, a flute, a tuba, cymbals, and a clarinet.

March! March!
March to the beat!

March! March!
Move those feet!

Patrick grabbed a baseball bat and Penny found an old sled with a long pulling strap.

18

BoBo's band now had a drum, a trumpet, a guitar, a flute, a tuba, cymbals, a clarinet, a trombone, and a keyboard.

March! March!
March to the beat!

March! March!
Move those feet!

BoBo and the band marched around the neighborhood.

Soon it was dinnertime. The band marched back to BoBo's house. Everyone put their instruments down and went home.

BoBo's garage was still a mess!

"BoBo, we can still help you clean," we told him. "Where should we start?"

"Well…" BoBo answered, "Let's go inside and start cleaning out the refrigerator. I'm **HUNGRY!**"

23

What instruments did BoBo and his neighbors play in BoBo's Band?

DRUM

TRUMPET

GUITAR

FLUTE

TUBA

CLARINET

CYMBALS

TROMBONE

KEYBOARD

Megan Burton got the inspiration for the BoBo Book Series while watching her father transition into the role of a fun-loving grandpa. The combination of growing up with an overly active imagination and influence from her father's unique sense of humor has encouraged her to write and share her sense of adventure for others to enjoy. Megan and her husband live in Michigan with their two energetic children who take them on adventures daily.

Dominic Wolocko is an accomplished artist having graduated with a BFA from Philadelphia College of Art with Honors. With over 30 years of experience, his illustrations have been published in the Philadelphia Inquirer, the Philadelphia Daily News, the Baltimore Sun, Science Digest, and Philadelphia Magazine. Dominic is a Detroit native currently living in Philadelphia with his husband. His family, consisting of 6 siblings, 13 nephews and nieces, and 20 great nephews and nieces, look forward to his personally drawn Christmas cards every year.

The character BoBo is based on Megan's father but Dominic is also Megan's uncle and BoBo's brother.